Short Stories

The Life of Charlie Ryan: A Squirrel's Tale

Sheralee Ryan

This paperback edition published 2020 by Jasami Publishing Ltd
an imprint of Jasami Publishing Ltd
Glasgow, Scotland
https://jasamipublishingltd.com

ISBN 978-1-913798-22-2

Acknowledgements

For Charlie who inspired me; also Gary and Keryn who believed in me.

Dedication

For Keryn Ryan who has an abundance of love for all God's creatures.

Contents

ZAMBIA

Prologue

The Adventures of Charlie Ryan are the real life encounters of a wild squirrel that came to live with the Ryan family in a small village called Kalumbila in the North West Province of Zambia. The adventures are true accounts as told and elaborated upon by Charlie's adopted Mom. This story aims to bring alive the emotions of animals into the lives of humans, so they too can be understood and accepted as beings that have as much right to live on our earth as does anyone else. This book is meant to give voice and hopefully a deeper understanding to this idea.

Charlie is a squirrel with a unique and fascinating personality. This story was written from his viewpoint in order to express thoughts, cares, dreams, passions, hurts, disappointments, and above all a love that goes beyond human ability.

Charlie's Family

Charlie's dad	Gary
Charlie's mom	Sheralee
Charlie's sister	Keryn
Dog brothers	Homer & Sheki (real brothers)
Dog sisters	Gazi and Nama
Cat sisters	Licorice and Blackie
Blind bird	Lilo
Owl	Bila
Owl	Kalum

Both Bila and Kalum were rehabilitated and released. All the injured wild animals who come to the Ryan home are released once they are completely rehabilitated.

Do You Know?

An owl has three eyelids: one for blinking, one for sleeping, and one for keeping the eye clean and healthy.

That Masuku are wild fruits that grow in Zambia. They are sweet-tasting, have a hard outside and a seed in the middle.

The Zambian bush is the uncultivated, wild foliage that covers the ground, and the tall trees higher than six men standing on each others shoulders reaching up to the sky. The untamed forest is home to the dangerous and venomous snakes as well other creatures that are unique to this area. There are anthills larger than a small house and during the rainy season all that is brown and dry turns to a lush green after the first downpour.

I Am Charlie Ryan

I am Charlie Ryan but sometimes Mom calls me Charlie B. I have no idea why she calls me that, but I love hearing her call my name. The "Ch" part sounds like "Sh". Sometimes when I'm in the top of the tallest trees in the garden and I hear Mom calling out my name loudly for all to hear, I hide just to listen to her calling and calling. It makes me so happy to hear my name being called.

I am a squirrel, by the way, and the only squirrel in our garden in fact in our village, that has a name. I love my name. I do come down from the trees to let Mom know where I am. I don't always go inside with her even when I know she wants me to. It seems she is happy to know where I am in the garden and once she spots me hanging upside down smiling at her she always smiles back and I feel so loved.

Then off she goes, back to whatever human moms do in their big houses, and leaves me to hang out in the beautiful tall trees.

Did I mention my mom is human? I'm adopted see. My squirrel mom met with an unfortunate end while saving me from a monstrous cat. It's hard to believe that horrid cat took my mother's life.

I have two sisters in my adopted family, they are cats. They are real lazy girls that sleep around all day long. I've tried so hard to play tag with them. and to jump on them when they are sleeping to see if they will give chase but they just move to somewhere else and carry on snoozing. Cats are no fun at all.

I also have four dog brothers and sisters. Two are real brothers and are super cool kids. They have so much energy just like I do but they can't climb trees. They try to, especially when other squirrels come to play, and we race up and down the trunks of the trees screaming at one another. They are called Homer and Sheki and are Fox Terriers. They run and jump as high as they can to reach the branches but they are just not made to climb trees.

Once, a big storm brought lots of rain and strong winds that blew the trees from side to side until one just snapped right down at its base. It crashed down over the fence and into the wild African bush next to us. Homer and Sheki were able to climb that tree pretty well. They hopped on from the garden side and ran all along to the other side where they hopped off and went for an adventure of their own in the wild bush. Mom was mad when she found them on the other side of the fence. They got themselves back home almost as quickly as they had left. Mom doesn't get mad often but when she does, she gets really mad.

I have a sister too. Her name is Keryn and she is the most beautiful human I have ever seen. She is kind, gentle, and so loving. She always gives me cuddles and kisses which makes me feel all tingly inside. Whatever Keryn has I am allowed to share with her. We drink milo together and share cookies, marshmallows, smarties, apples, or grapes.

You name it, if I can eat it, Keryn will share with me. In her room there is a big shelf filled with toy animals that are soft and cuddly. I sleep in there whenever I want to but not at night. During the night I have to sleep in my own bed in my own room with the door and the window shut. Mom says it's to keep me safe because there are creatures of the night like Gracie the awful cat who killed my squirrel mom. Even though I know the story of my real mom I am such a happy squirrel in my adopted home.

I also have another sister who was saved a long time ago. She is a bulbul or toppie; which is a bird for those of you who don't know what that is. Her story is rather scary too. Huge baboons came and tore up her home when she was just the other side of being an egg. I don't quite understand the egg part. I don't think I would like to be called an egg at any time of my life. Lilo sits in an open cage with all her food bowls and water lined up in the same order every day because she is blind. She cannot see a thing! She doesn't know what I look like. I told her I am the most handsome squirrel in Kalumbila and she believes me!

When the dustbin truck comes on a Monday and a Thursday all the dogs race to the gate and shout and scream at the dustbin collectors. No one has a clue what they are shouting, not even themselves! Lilo whistles as loudly as she can and they all stop their ruckus and come running back inside.

So now you have met all my family members except my dad. He is big and tall and not around much except for two days of the week. I think that's called the weekend, because I know he goes to work on all the other days. He leaves before I wake up in the morning and some nights I am asleep before he gets home. I try to keep awake as long as I can so I can see him and when I do I race up his leg and onto his shoulder and back down the other side. It makes him laugh and jump and dance about. My dad lets me stay up longer just to play with me but some nights I am so tired from my adventures outside that I just have to go curl up in my soft warm bed and go to sleep. Mom comes and tucks me in every night and kisses me on my head. I love my family.

The Scary Tunnel

In the mornings I usually wake up with a nice big stretch and a really big yawn. I check to see what fresh treats have been put down for me and then I go look for my family to say good morning and find out who wants to play.

Blackie and Licorice, my lazy cat sisters, are usually still asleep somewhere. I wonder when they eat! I eat a lot. I love food and can spend an entire day in a tree looking for the perfect berry or fruit. You have to try each one you find even if it doesn't look that good. It's all in the taste.

There is a tree in the corner of our garden close to the vegetable garden and at one time it was absolutely covered in small figs.

I spent nearly a week visiting that tree until I found the perfect fig. I also discovered that the trunk of that tree is hollow inside right up to the top. Then I found out that it gets quite tight in there after a week-long feast of figs. I went in on the first day and made a few noises. An echo came back and it sounded as though I had an old voice that was speaking right back at me. I scared myself a little and shot back out and up the outside of the trunk taking lots of short breaths to take in all the air I could.

That's when I heard Mom calling my name and, on that day, I sprinted across the lawn hardly even touching the grass with my little pink feet, and played inside for the rest of the day. I heard Mom say that I was such a clever squirrel and a really good boy for coming so quickly when I was called. She didn't know I scared myself silly making creepy noises in the dark tunnel of the fig tree trunk. Nor does she know that the tree spoke back to me.

The next day I took a while deciding if I should go there or not. I hung around poking Blackie until I got her to move then went and did the same to Licorice.

I played with Keryn racing up and down the back of her chair and onto her books. I took her pencil and had a good chew on the end. I've seen her do that sometimes when she is thinking hard. She laughed and got a new one, so I thought that maybe what she was doing is quite important and I shouldn't interrupt her too much.

I heard Mom ask how her schoolwork is going. I don't go to people school. I think I'm too cool for school. As a squirrel, I'll learn all I need to learn about life out in the trees.

I eventually did go back to the fig tree and stayed out in the sunshine looking and tasting and throwing figs down to the ground. Homer came to see what I was up to. He can be nosey like that sometimes. I threw figs at him and he couldn't figure out how I managed to hit him on the head every time no matter where he moved to. Homer isn't as clever as he thinks he is! It was fun for a while but Homer got bored and went somewhere else with Sheki.

They are always together planning and plotting what they might do next. They love wrestling each other and tumbling around on the lawn. I would love to play like that with them but Mom won't let them play rough with me. She thinks I might get hurt.

After a week of figs, I had almost forgotten about the inside passage of the tree and when I did remember I actually had the courage to go back in. That was even more scary than the first time. I almost got stuck because my belly had got bigger and I had to squeeze back down tail first because I couldn't even make a turn.

So that settled things forever after. No more going inside trees. I will stick to the outside and that's final. Unless I'm being chased, and if whoever is chasing me isn't playing but wants me for dinner then I will definitely break my rule and go in; I say that will be allowed. That's the rule!

A Mystery To Be Solved

One day Dad came home earlier than he usually does. There was so much excitement in the air that I could feel it from the tippy top of the tallest tree in the garden. I raced down to the bottom at breakneck speed and hopped through the window only to see Dad on his way back out shouting as he strode down the driveway, "be careful for Charlie hey!" Mom muttered under her breath and disappeared into Keryn's bathroom, closing the door behind her.

I knew something was up, so I hung around the veranda pretending to be busy with cleaning my face and checking my tail. The dogs were all lying outside the bathroom door as if Mom was preparing treats in there for them. They never know what's going on. Gazi thinks she knows it all just because she is the oldest but if you ask her a question, she just looks at you and moves her eyebrows around while everything else stays still. It's a cool trick but it doesn't answer questions.

Nama is always scared and a real pessimist if ever there was one. She thinks the world is coming to an end if her supper is five minutes late!

The boys, Homer and Sheki, argued about who could get closest to the door without touching the other. They almost got into a massive squabble but Mom opened the door and told them to go away. They didn't, they never listen but they did settle down. Dogs can be boring. They will wait and wait and wait for something to happen. I, on the other hand, do not.

So, I left to find a treat to snack on while all was calm and quiet. We have a fish tank in our lounge. They are our pets, I think. I've heard strangers come to our house saying they want to see our pets, but they never ever look at the fish tank which I find quite strange. They look at me mostly which can be annoying.

One day a kid came to the house. I don't always like strangers and Mom said I don't have to like everybody. So, when this kid came and stared at me, I took off. I went to the very highest end of the closest tree I could get to, and I refused to come down. It is so amazing up there, all the humans look smaller, about the same size as me, and so I feel better dealing with ones I don't like from up there.

I also found the last of my favourite seed pods up there and they are even better baked by the sun, all dried up and crispy.

That reminded me that I was going to visit the fish tank while Mom was in the bathroom. I went to see it and found the most foul-smelling plastic bottle with no way in. How silly is that? I chewed a little hole in the side to see what could possibly have died in there, and I found dried up and crispy paper-like seeds that were very stinky! The fish were all in a tizzy going up and down the side of the tank as if they actually wanted this rotten flaky stuff.

If a fish had a tongue like a dog these fish would be licking the glass to get to the stinky stuff. So, I puckered up, squeezed my eyes shut and tasted the tiniest possible amount just to find out what they were on about. Oh my, that was so gross! I cannot believe they wanted it so much. I threw the fish tub down and the food made a mess everywhere. The fish can have it! Then I ran to my water bowl to rinse and gargle and spit.

Out the window of my bedroom I noticed Blackie and Licorice having a private little cat conference so I hopped out to see what it was all about. They stopped whispering as soon as they saw me and went off in opposite directions. I just knew something was up, and it somehow involved me. Dad's warning "be careful for Charlie" kept ringing in my ears.

I thought it best to hang about the house to see if I could figure this mystery out. I must have fallen asleep under the sofa and woke up with a dog snoring too close to my ear! Mom was in the kitchen cutting stuff up into small pieces and putting it into one of the cat's bowls, then she started off towards the bathroom. I ran behind her and climbed up her leg so I could go with her. I desperately needed to see what was behind that bathroom door.

Keryn came and fetched me but I squealed and wriggled and freed myself just in time to run back and see through the half-opened door into the bathroom. There on the floor sat a huge spotted eagle owl. I looked at him with my eyes wide and my mouth open and he looked at me with one big eye. There was an owl in our house!

A Visitor To Our Garden

After getting over the shock of seeing such a big, beautiful owl actually inside our house, I realised he had been hurt and my family had brought him home to take care of him just like they had done with me and with little Lilo. They are like that, my family. They love God's creatures and care for them when they need to be cared for, just like this owl. His name is Kalum and Mom says if his injuries are not too serious, he will get better and go back to the forest where he lives.

What my mom doesn't know is that once one of God's creatures comes into our house, they become a Ryan and they don't want to go back to where they came from. I know this because one day when I was out in the garden scratching around in the fork of a tall tree a very large, spotted eagle owl landed next to me. I got such a fright that I hopped nearly all the way back to last week Sunday.

After she had settled on the branch next to me, she spoke softly and calmly. Her voice was mesmerising and I could have listened to her all day. She told me that a long time ago she also had come to our house with an injured eye that took three months to heal. All that time she was looked after and loved by Keryn and Mom. She told me her name was Bila.

Owls need to catch their own food and Bila had a family on the other side of the dam so although she didn't want to leave, she needed to get back to her mate. Bila said that she didn't visit often, only when she could and it was just to get a feel of the love she so well remembered from when she stayed in our house. I know all about that love.

Once I found my voice, I told Bila my story and she turned her head and looked at me with the biggest roundest eyes; they reminded me of deep pools of dark water. Nothing seemed wrong with her eyes at all and I told her so. She admitted that she was better long before she let the humans know she was ready to go and quite honestly, she didn't want to go.

She stayed in the garden on a fallen down tree by the anthill and Keryn sat next to her until it started to get dark. She knew Keryn needed to get back inside, and also knew if she didn't fly off Keryn would stay there next to her on that fallen down tree all night long.

Bila blinked and I saw only one eye got covered over with the eyelid that has feathers on it. Her injury must have been pretty bad. Bila was a very wise owl and she warned me of the yellow billed kites. They would eat squirrels for breakfast, lunch, and dinner if they could and there are a lot of them here where we live. Bila promised to let the word out that I was special and might need protection. She would mention also that I eat too much junk food and would probably not taste very good. Apparently, yellow billed kites are health conscious and only like organic foods; whatever that is. I'm very happy I'm not organic. Anyway, I don't want to take any chances. They won't know how I taste until they taste me and I don't fancy anyone taking a bite out of me.

Bila looked tired and she asked me to please excuse her while she took a nap. She wanted to wait in my tree for my Dad to come home so she could see him too. She loves my family just as much as I do and that is quite a lot of love. I raced down the tree to call Mom to come and see Bila but Jordan, the guy who works in our garden every now and then, had already told her to come see. She ran to the tall tree and told me to go inside to Keryn. Mom was so happy to see Bila she took a hundred photographs and I heard her on the phone telling Dad the exciting news.

Bila stayed in the tree all that day and waited for Dad to get home from work. She flew lower down in the tree and Mom and Dad stood together looking up at Bila calling her name and sending her all the love that they could. As the sun went down, Bila flew off in the direction of the dam where her mate was expecting her to come home.

The Smartie Tree

It rains here sometimes and I don't really like climbing wet trees, because my feet don't seem to stick all that well to bark when it is wet.

One day it was raining so hard and it had come on so suddenly that I didn't have time to find shelter, so I sat in the tree wondering what to do. Mom came out wearing a very big hat with a handle so it didn't have to sit on her head. I bet it was too big for her head and that's why she had to hold it by the handle part. It seemed to work quite well and kept her dry. What a funny sight it was!

It reminded me of the giant mushrooms that grow in the forest here and I wondered if that was where Mom got the idea to hold one over her head when it rains. I decided the next giant mushroom would be mine.

Hopefully, I'll find one on a rainy day just like today. I ran along the grass next to Mom but once I got to the verandah I was soaked to the skin. Mom said I looked like a drowned rat and so she dried me off and put me into my warm cozy bed to warm up.

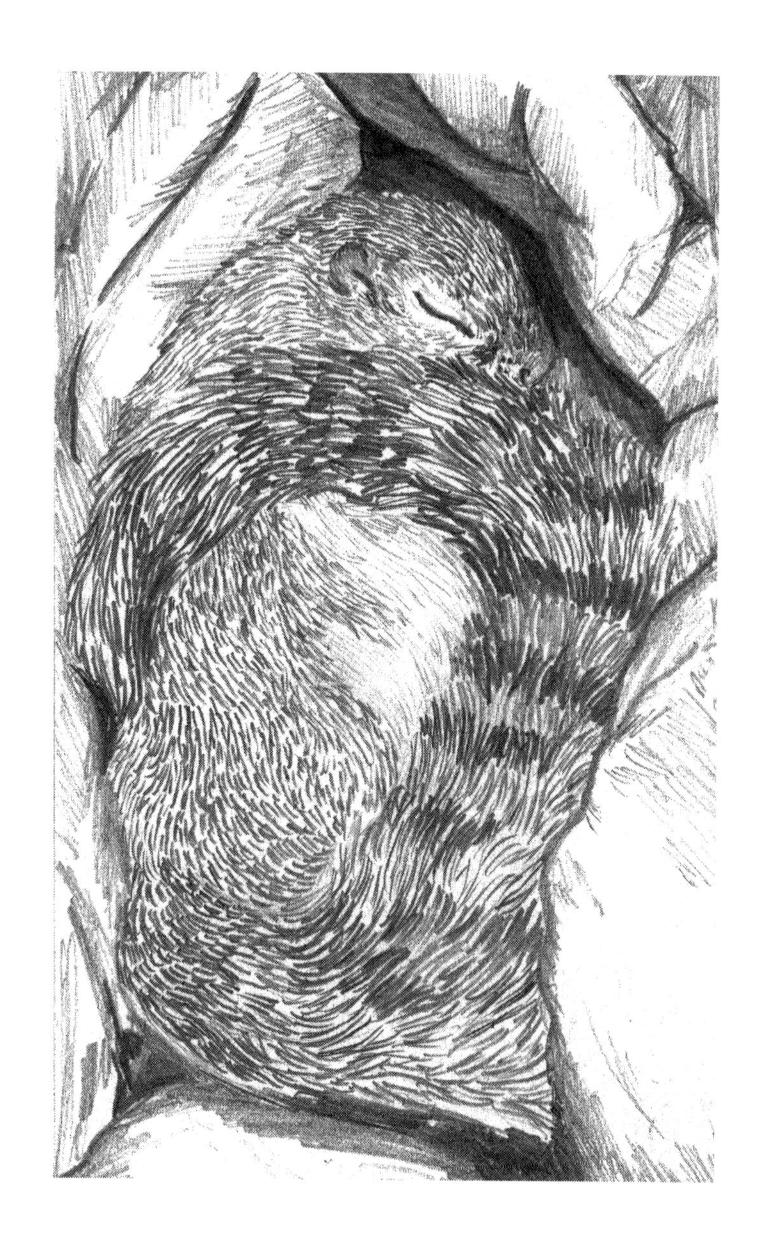

Squirrels don't like getting wet and they dislike being cold even more. I am such a lucky squirrel to have soft, warm blankets to curl up in and sleep on during cold, rainy days. Keryn also does not like cold, rainy days because she has to stay indoors, and we often spend those in-door days together.

She makes us a big mug of hot milo to share and even puts in a marshmallow just for me. Keryn loves me so much and is always spoiling me with special treats. She has taught me how to share. Squirrels don't really like sharing. If they have any extra Smarties or nuts, they would rather hide them from other squirrels and save them for when they feel like eating them again. The only problem with this is, how easy it is to forget good hiding places.

I once hid a Smartie up on the curtain rail and only found it a week or so later. It had faded to white with purplish spots but it still tasted just like a Smartie, so I ate it up there on the curtain rail. I love Smarties.

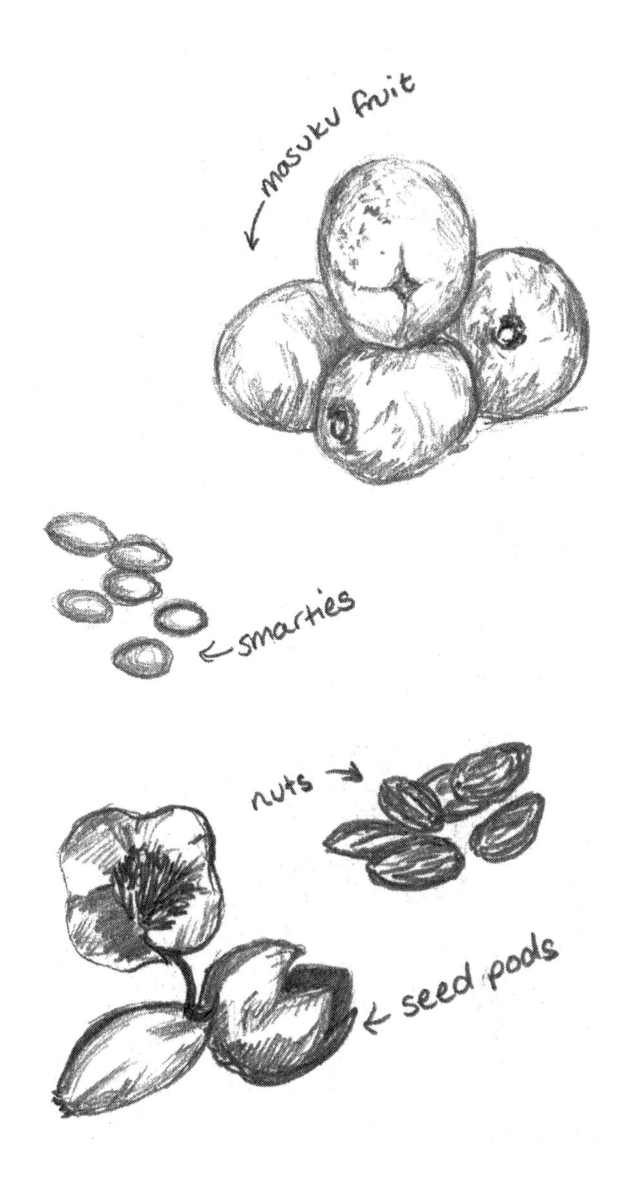
masuku fruit
smarties
nuts
seed pods

There is a masuku tree in our garden and every day that is not a rainy day I go out to check if there are any masuku. I know when I first started learning to climb trees the masuku tree was covered in fruit and there were lots of squabbles when other squirrels came to look for the perfect masuku. I was scared of heights then and hadn't mastered my tree climbing skills but I didn't miss out because my mom asked Jordan to pick the best masuku he could find for me so I could have them where I felt safe. Now the masuku season is over and I can climb like a pro but there aren't any masuku!

We have so many trees in our garden and there are delicious treats on nearly all of them at different times of the year. One thing I still haven't found though is the Smartie tree and I do wonder where Mom goes to pick them. I will keep on searching until I find a Smartie tree.

It has been lovely being able to share my life and my adventures with you and I hope you have enjoyed reading about me. For now,

I'm off to start a new adventure and hope to share it with you all in good time. With much love as always from my little squirrel heart to yours…

Charlie Ryan

Charlie's

Photo Gallery

Beautiful Bila

Bottle Baby

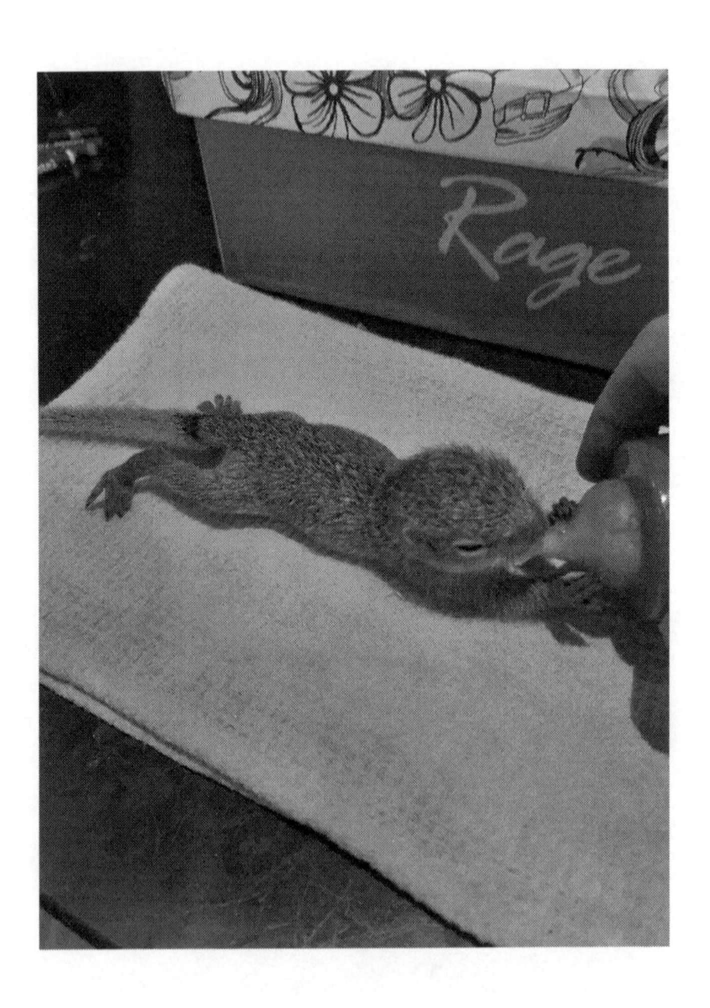

Flat Out After A Hard Day Snacking

From The Smartie Tree

Siblings - Homer, Sheki, and Gazi

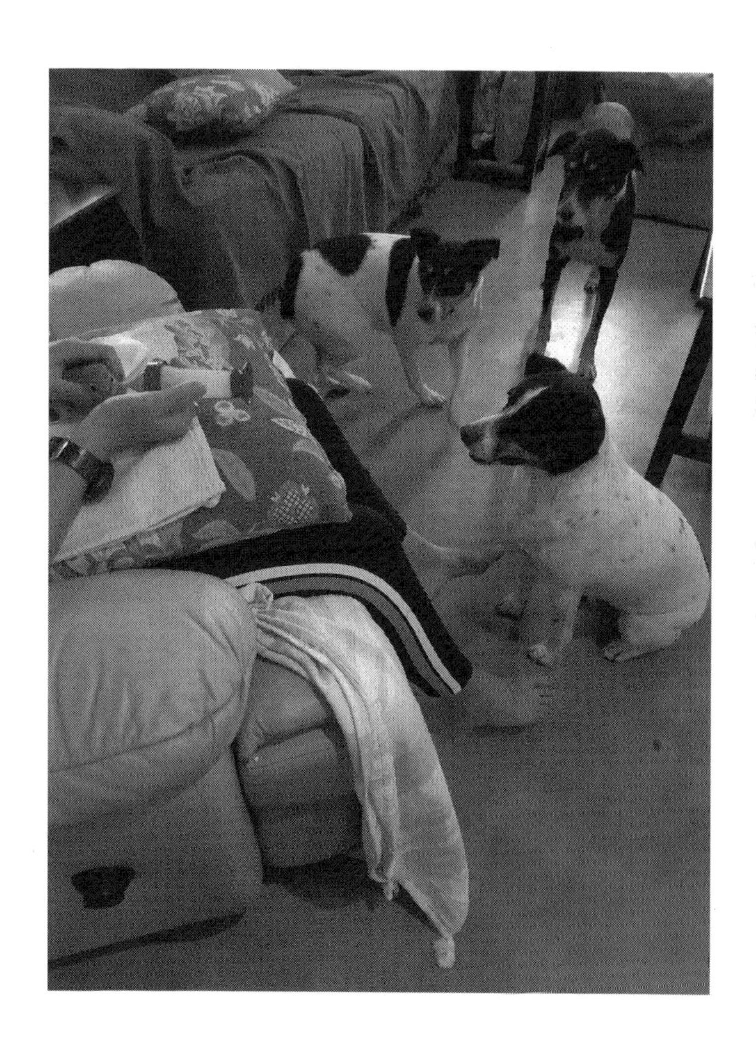

I Found A Family

I Want To Go Golfing Dad

In The Garden

Just Hanging Around

Lovely Lilo

Mom You're Too Funny!

Snack Time!

Squirrels Don't Share

Time For Snuggles

Up A Tree! Look At Me!

What Is It Mom?

About the Author

Originally from Durban, South Africa Sheralee, her husband Gary and young daughter Keryn moved to Namibia where they stayed for almost six years. Always having had a love for nature and God's beautiful creatures, Namibia provided the opportunity for the Ryan family to experience wildlife first hand. For the first two years, they lived in a cottage on a fish farm on the Zambezi River. In 2015 the family moved on to Gobabis, 200 kilometres east of Windhoek where they were involved with the Gobabis Animal Rescue, helping and caring for animals in need. At the end of 2018, they moved to Kalumbila, North West Province of Zambia where their interaction with nature continues and, where possible, they have assisted injured animals, to rehabilitate and release them back into the wild. Charlie's amazing personality inspired Sheralee to write his story, from his point of view naturally.

Other Works

For The Latest Information On

What is Available

New Releases

&

Coming Soon

Please Visit

JasamiPublishingLtd.com